Ava Sky
ADVENTURER

Written by Kath Reynolds

Illustrated by Taylor Barron

Collins

1 Leaving my cocoon

Hi! I'm Ava Skye, loving cat owner and enthusiastic adventurer.

OK, I'm not adventuring *all* the time.

My routine is important to me, too.

Doing certain things in the same way helps me feel comfortable, confident and safe:

- Waking up at 6 o'clock.

- Wearing clothes that don't itch or feel too tight.

- Eating tomato sandwiches for breakfast and dinner. Loads of foods smell bad and feel weird in my mouth, but not tomato sandwiches! They make every molecule in me smile.
- Dancing with my cat, Amelia Earhart, after dinner.
- Getting into bed at 8 o'clock, and reading until I fall asleep.

Still, the days I love most are those I set aside to try something new. Once a week, I exchange my comfy routine for the thrill of not knowing what comes next. On those days, I feel like a butterfly leaving a cocoon, spreading my wings for the first time.

Today is one of those days!

2 The Adventure Hat

It used to take me forever to choose a new adventure.
So one day, while deciding whether to put on a play
or do karaoke, my grampa intervened and gave me
the best gift ever.

A fancy antique I call, *The Adventure Hat*!

Gramps bought it in a shop of old stuff that smells like a million yesterdays. Gramps and his brother had a hat just like it as kids and it stopped them from arguing over which game to play. They wrote down suggestions and took turns picking from the hat. Gramps thought an "ideas hat" might help me, too.

I've already jotted down hundreds of adventure suggestions. All I have to do is pick one to try next.

Roller skating?

I've always wanted to go roller skating!

It's just ... I have an overwhelming fear that I'll fall.

So I stim. I bounce my legs and pick my fingers as I imagine myself crashing to the ground in front of strangers.

Then I think back on my previous conquests, remembering how I was nervous to try them too. But in the end, it all worked out.

It's hard to remember these things sometimes, so Gramps and I wrote some "Rules for Adventuring" to look back on when I'm feeling nervous or afraid.

Rules
for
ADVENTURING

Rule 1:

Keep in mind that sometimes being an adventurer means feeling excited and scared all at once.

I keep Rule 1 in mind and focus on what I need to do next. If I'm going roller skating, I'll need some skates!

3 Feet fear!

I call my best friend Mako. I'm sure his sister has skates.

"Does Lira have roller skates I could borrow?"

"I think so," Mako answers. "Wait … You picked roller skating from the hat today, didn't you?"

"Want to come with me?"

Mako gasps. "You know I'm always up for an adventure!"

Lira has skates … and everything else, too. Why does she think I need so much protective gear? I bang my knuckles together and bite my lip, worrying. She must know I'm going to fall. I shake off the thought and grab Lira's skates to try on.

Usually I won't wear other people's shoes.
Just thinking of strange sweaty feet makes me cringe.
But Lira's skates are brand new and that's good enough for me.

But … "They're too big!"

Mako worries too. "I have pads and wrist guards, but no skates."

"That's OK," says Gramps. "There are rental skates at the rink."

My stomach sours. I pace Mako's hallway, slamming my hand against my thigh, trying to gather my thoughts. All I can picture are a thousand smelly, moist feet inside the skates I'll have to wear.

What if sweat trapped in the skates leaks through my socks and into my skin?

What if previous skaters had itchy, oozing rashes and *I* get an itchy, oozing rash?

"Remember when I refused to hold that humungous spider in Mr Hanson's class and you told me, 'You never have to do anything you're not ready to do'?" asks Mako.

Rule 2:
You never have to do anything you're not ready to do.

I sigh. "I remember. Rule 2."

"Why did you make that rule?"

I smile. "Because when you force yourself to do something you're not ready to do, it's not fun anymore. It's just another chore."

Mako grins. "Exactly."

I think everything over and come to a decision.
"I refuse to let other people's feet stop our fun."

"To the roller rink!" Gramps exclaims.

"To the roller rink!" Mako and I shout.

4 Let's skate!

It's official: the roller rink is the best place on Earth.

There's only one problem …

The music is *way* too loud.

BOOM-BOOM-BOOM!

Each note pounds through my skin and rattles my bones. I cover my ears, but it doesn't help. The noise gets bigger and bigger, until it almost sweeps me away.

Then I remember:

My earbuds!

Rule 3:
Adventurers must come prepared.

"Looking for these?" Gramps hands me my noise-cancelling earbuds. I put them in and sigh with relief. The blaring music and chatter of the crowd mutes just enough to hear the songs, Mako and Gramps.

"Thanks, Gramps."

Now I can focus on getting my skates.

The skate hire counter is busy. When it's our turn, I ask the man how many feet have been inside their skates.

"A few. But don't worry. We disinfect and clean our skates after each use so they're good as new."

Whew! That helps my stinky-foot anxiety. Better still, they have my favourite colours: green and blue.

Let's get ready to roll!

18

Gramps buys snacks while we put on our skates and protective gear.

When we're ready, Mako and I leap out of the booth without thinking. Our wheels roll out from under us. Our arms fly into the air. Suddenly, all the fears I had about falling come true.

Time slows. My whole life flashes before my eyes. Family, laughter, friends, so many delicious tomato sandwiches and memories dance through my mind as I fall.

5 Shuffle, boom, fly!

My teeth rattle in my skull when I hit the ground.
But when I assess myself for damage, I realise I'm OK.

I fell. But I survived.

I turn to Mako. "Are you all right?"

Mako nods. "A little sore, but nothing serious, thanks
to these wrist guards. You?"

I nod. "Lira was right about needing all this gear.
Shame we didn't have bottom-guards, too!"
Mako laughs as I help him up. "Ready to try again?"

"*So* ready!"

We shuffle towards the rink. I concentrate on my feet and how the wheels move. I try to enjoy the moment and not get anxious about skaters rushing by. But as more people crowd the rink, this is extra stressful.

"Everyone knows what they're doing," Mako says, "except us."

"I guess they were all new to roller skating once, too. It's hard to get our moves right, at first. But at least now we know that if we fall, we'll get back up again. Right?"

Mako holds his head higher. "Right."

Mako and I half-walk, half-skate onto the rink.
I stumble and grab the rail. But after a few rounds,
I roll smoother. Faster. More confidently.

I find a space in the crowd. I pump my arms to
go faster. The wind blows my hair back. I feel as
free as a hawk soaring over the sky. In this moment,
I don't care how many feet were in these skates
before mine, or how many people whirl around me.
I feel great! When I pass Gramps, I wave
with both hands …

… and knock myself off balance. The rubber tip on my skate catches the floor. I jerk backwards. My earbuds fly.

Boom. I land on my tailbone, but the loud music hurts more. I crawl after my earbuds and put them back in.

Some children laugh when I try to get up. I shrink with embarrassment. People laughing at me makes me feel like a colourful bird in a monochrome world. Like I don't belong.

But when I see Mako rushing towards me, I remember who I am and why I'm here.

I'm Ava Skye. I make my own rules and belong right here!

6 New friend

"Ava!" Mako rolls to my side. "My turn to help you?"

"Yes please," I catch my balance and lean on the rail.

Like Rule 4 for Adventuring says:

We all need a little help sometimes.

Before I push off, someone catches my eye.

Rule 4:
Always be ready to offer or accept help.

26

I roll over to a scared-looking boy. "Hi. I'm Ava."

Mako waves. "I'm Mako. Do you need help?"

"I'm Bashir," the boy says. "I've never skated before."

"Really?" I say. "Today's our first time, too."

Mako gives Bashir a friendly smile and we hold out our elbows. "Would you like to join us?"

Bashir grins and takes our arms. "Yes please."

The three of us skate for another hour as Gramps eats ice cream with Bashir's dad.

I skate so fast, I fly. And this time, I don't fall!

Back home, I document today's expedition in my journal, then think up more things I'd like to try and add them to my hat. Afterwards, I slip back into my comfortable routine and dream about new adventures.

Until next time, this is Ava Skye, Adventurer ... over and out!

Rules for Adventuring

Rule 1:

Keep in mind that sometimes being an adventurer means feeling excited and scared all at once.

roller skating

Rule 2:

You never have to do anything you're not ready to do.

Rule 3:

Adventurers must come prepared.

Rule 4:

Always be ready to offer or accept help.

 Ideas for reading

Written by Gill Matthews
Primary Literacy Consultant

Reading objectives:
- check that the text makes sense to them, discussing their understanding and explaining the meaning of words in context
- ask questions to improve their understanding of a text
- draw inferences such as inferring characters' feelings, thoughts and motives from their actions, and justify inferences with evidence

Spoken language objectives:
- ask relevant questions to extend their understanding and knowledge
- use relevant strategies to build their vocabulary
- articulate and justify answers, arguments and opinions

Curriculum links: Relationships education – Respectful relationships; English – Writing – composition

Interest words: excited, scared, prepared, accept

Build a context for reading

- Discuss the front cover, challenging children to identify some of the objects shown. Read the title and ask children what it means to them.
- Read the back-cover blurb. Ask children what they think might happen in the story.
- Explore any unfamiliar vocabulary and support children in working out the meaning of the words.
- Ask children about their experiences of roller skating.

Understand and apply reading strategies

- Read pp2–5 aloud using the punctuation and meaning to help you read with appropriate expression.
- Discuss the character Ava Skye, exploring children's impressions of her. Encourage them to support their responses with reasons and evidence from the text.